Fresh Hell

Motherhood in Pieces

Carellin Brooks

DEMETER

DEMETER PRESS, BRADFORD, ONTARIO

Canada Council   Conseil des Arts
for the Arts   du Canada

The publisher gratefully acknowledges the support of the Canada Council for the Arts for its publishing program.

Demeter Press logo based on the sculpture "Demeter"
by Maria-Luise Bodirsky <www.keramik-atelier.bodirsky.de>

Printed and Bound in Canada

Front cover: Finn Canadensis, Honk Honk Graphic Arts

Library and Archives Canada Cataloguing in Publication

Brooks, Carellin, author
    Fresh hell: motherhood in pieces / Carellin Brooks.

ISBN 978-1-927335-32-1

Cataloguing data available from Library and Archives Canada.

Demeter Press
140 Holland Street West
P. O. Box 13022
Bradford, ON L3Z 2Y5
Tel: (905) 775-9089
Email: info@demeterpress.org
Website: www.demeterpress.org

for my girls

Contents

Acknowledgements

First and foremost, I would like to thank my daughters, for putting up with me. They are each far better than I deserve. My heartfelt thanks also to Peter Nosco for all those plates of food, and especially for the extra hours of sleep. I would also like to thank those who provided invaluable advice, kind and sensitive comments, subtitle suggestions, and lucid queries, not necessarily in that order, namely Angie Chan, Kyla Epstein, Daniel Gawthrop, Brett Josef Grubisic, John Harris, Vivien Lougheed, Melva McLean, Julia Saunders and the members of Letterheads: Mindy Abramowitz, Kate Bird, and Shannon Underwood. Finally, my thanks to everyone at Demeter Press, especially Andrea O'Reilly, and to Finn Canadensis, cover designer extraordinaire!

1. Surprise

WHEN A BABY HAS THE BIG ONE, the special, the surprise, you can't help but feel tricked. You're stripping off what appears to be a perfectly ordinary diaper. There are no ominous musical chords, nothing to warn you. The baby too is perfectly ordinary, screeching or waving its arms agreeably depending upon the time of day, alignment of the stars, alien messages being piped into its baby brain and other factors you will never in a million years comprehend.

Then you catch it. Your first glimpse. No, you say. Like a child you comfort yourself: you imagined it, everything's fine. But as you continue to peel back the diaper you morph into a horror-film heroine, sheer white nightgown and all, starting down the shadowy cellar stairs with inadequate candlestick in hand.

Now it's the audience that hears those ominous chords, wills you to go back, slam the door and bar it for good measure. Here your own body and brain attain a rare unity; your own senses yell at you to refasten the Velcro, turn around, go out the door and don't come back. Because down there, It awaits. The Blob. Viscous, pitiless, spackling baby's crevices and oozing out the sides. And now comes the first sly waft of a miasma that will soon enough fill up the room, creamy and soured: your sweet milk turned dark.

Wrappings unpeeled, you face it at last: the horror. Every inch of formerly pristine cotton (and you decided to use cloth, you self-righteous fool you; now look what you've done) is coated in Harvest Gold. Then the creases, each one to be swabbed. The outrage. The insult. And even as you gape and gasp the baby continues to goo, untroubled by the sensation of cold poo packed into its backside like a perverse beauty treatment and utterly unconscious of the great wrong it just committed. Why should baby care? It's your problem now. You're looking around for the candid camera, waiting for the punchline, wondering how long before the curtain rises and someone arrives to say it's all a joke and nobody in their right mind would expect you to clean up that horror. That hell.

So when there's no reprieve, no laughing audience, nothing to do but face the thick and evilly scented facts and mop up as best you can, you go in search of your fellow sinner. Would a responsible parent take it out on the baby? After all, you are, or should be, happy she delivered what appears to be the entire contents of her intestines to your unwilling attentions. Think of the alternative. Best not wonder if they even make tubing that small. So now it's down to him. Your loved one, your dearest, your darling, that prick. Not the baby's father, true, but near enough: anyway, he's around now and you have nobody else to blame. See, you definitely have something to say, not about the shit—of course that's not his fault, any rational person knows that—but about the diaper bucket. How he's thoughtlessly placed it too far from the bed, or too close to it. The lack of a change table itself a reliably picked bone. If only he'd agreed to drive to Abbotsford that night, get the one off Craigslist, who cares if it was midnight, didn't he understand about the baby's need for modular furniture, your needs? And speaking of needs, you add, as you round the doorway and catch him mid-act, what the hell is he doing thoughtlessly answering his email at seven o'clock at night, instead of divining this emergency and rushing to assist: boiling tub, swabbing cloths, hazmat suit?

And as your voice rises, there in the doorway, you hear the voices of all the women before you, querulous, harsh, rich with complaint. And you understand this isn't about the baby, about the missing washcloths or about how he spends his time. It's about the great cosmic injustice of everything. Other people are lining up at restaurants where the hostesses are really nice and wearing makeup even, imagine, the kids are using some app you've never even heard of, much less figured out, gals like your neighbour you've never met are getting into cabs at nine o'clock in the morning wearing mirrored sunglasses and beige pants—you saw her, this very morning, doing that very thing, and for a long time afterwards you would have killed to be her, going to Cancun on a cheap package deal, heading for the airport, eating breakfast out. That would be the answer, wouldn't it, just escape, just get away from it all.

And as you slam the door on his pissed-off back and, gazing satisfied into the bathroom mirror, discover the source of the lingering smell in a swipe of violently mustard-coloured poo above one eyebrow, you remember: This is what you've always wanted.

2. Conceived Of

I WANT ANOTHER BABY, you'd said.

You'd been saying so for years. *Wait*, said all the couples counsellors and marital therapists you consulted before, throughout, and in the midst of the spectacular flameout of your failed marriage. *There's plenty of time. I'm not sure it's such a good idea*, said your loved one, when the two of you had dated a while and come close enough to talk about your futures. *For your career. I don't want another baby*, said your older daughter, looking around the small place where you lived. *Where would it sleep?*

You didn't have plenty of time. You knew you couldn't wait. Your age, for one: you noticed anew the articles in the paper, written as it were especially for you. The decline of fertility as one aged, on a graph, like a cliff face. The increased chromosonal risks peaking in the opposite direction: Down syndrome, birth defects, idiocy.

And then you wanted another for the same reason teenage girls do—to have something of your own. Your first child's life had evolved into a skein of messy arrangements and compromises: the visits with your ex, not to mention the father's new romance, inconveniently conceived elsewhere and thus necessitating extended out-of-town visits. You'd at least avoid that nibbling hell this time. You thirsted to make all the decisions yourself, even if they turned out wrong.

Eventually you realized that if nobody agreed with your plan neither could they stop you. Figuring this out took years. You realized that if you lied and said you had enough money to support another baby no officials would demand proof. The technologies of assisted reproduction had their advantages. Conception would be clean, as they described it at the clinic. The child, if you succeeded, coming to you an almost perfect mystery, parentage an answered questionnaire accompanied by a picture of a man you'd never meet, the donor. Reproduction isolated from the messy world of human relationships, the fragile bond with your loved one that could stick this time or, like the others, unpredictably unravel. So you went to the clinic, and you paid your money, and you got what you wanted.

You had never married or even lived with the father of your firstborn and you certainly didn't intend to marry or live with your loved one, who wasn't even the second one's father. Not now, at least. Later, maybe. He talked vaguely of moving. He lived across town, in a big place, and you lived downtown, in a little one. You'd been together a while now. You each liked your places fine. As for each other's they at least had the charm of novelty. You'd go back and forth, with the baby. The details would resolve themselves. That's what you thought, while you waited for the donor's sperm to take. And after the baby, that's what happened. It worked just like you'd imagined. For a while. *I'll do anything,* your loved one said early on, *except change diapers.* Fair enough. Your decision, your responsibility. It worked on paper. It wasn't his fault, the exhausting reality, no easier even though you'd known how it would be. Was it?

3. Immaculate

THE BABY WASN'T ALWAYS a mere producer of appalling effluvia. There was a time, believe it or not, when it represented more than an apparently endless string of unpleasant chores. Then the baby was a real baby: soft and sweet and most charmingly inert, unaware of its own orifices and their potential to produce horrors almost beyond description. Days passed with it nestled up against you, breathing into your neck without upchucking, its eyes blissfully closed almost continuously. It was the size of a family tin of Libby's tomato juice. You popped it into a folded sling like a letter into a slot and carried it with you wherever you went, next to your heart. Your special delivery had arrived, everything you'd imagined. Fluffy kittens, sunsets, rainbows: nothing compared to this glowing bundle of pure peace, dandelion puff hope, dream taken flesh.

That's when you were a real mother. Then you could coo and caress and share a rapturous glance with your loved one, at what you alone had produced. Your story, writ small. When you could trace the line of tiny lashes against its downy cheek, unmarred except for that acne they all seemed to get, and surreptitiously rub at the scruff on its scalp. Cradle crap. Marvel at its tiny nails. You know. Baby book stuff.

That moment, alas, lasted all of three weeks. Now you're stuck. Years to come of this, all because of your foolishness, your failure (as you put it to him, accusingly) to think things through. Predict the consequences. Understand the basic laws of cause and effect.

Well, you wanted it, he says, using that tone you liked, in the days you could access sensations between numb and infuriated. Pre-baby, you must have had the energy to toss your hair and laugh gaily, as you accepted another overlarge drink. Sitting on the sofa in his living room, looking out over the strait.

4. Natural Disasters

BABY CURLED BESIDE YOU IN BED, rise and fall of small clothes, you give up to wonder. In a famine, would your milk dry up, or continue even as you shriveled to rack and ruin? Who should die first: you to save it, it for you to have more? There must be a rough calculus in our DNA: self-preservation or, conversely, perpetuation of the species. It's all biological, after all. Maybe the airlines have it figured: secure your own mask first.

A teenage girl on the bus explains to her friends that babies are cute so we don't kill them. Maybe she doesn't say this, maybe she just says leave them behind. You have trouble re-membering these days. Periods of static as with a badly tuned radio, buzzing times where everything intelligible fades. Could sleep deprivation alone cause this imbecility? Maybe instead it's early-onset Alzheimer's, a brain tumour. Risk factors: aluminum in your fillings, mercury-riddled sushi, bearing a baby at an advanced age. Then the hazards of home: fluoride, lead pipes, carbon monoxide. Could there be a cleaning product you've forgotten to swap out for some ineffective nature brand or purported home equivalent? Then the bath, where you could be slathering yourself with poison that works its way into your system, ending up in the milk ducts and giving your baby autism? Ah, autism, something else to worry about.

If the building caught fire would you throw the baby out first in the hopes that someone would catch it, or would you hold it and jump and if so, would you be able to twist your body in midair so as to land underneath? An intruder comes in the front door: would it be best to go out the window even though there's a locked gate outside, effectively trapping you? What if you were in a boat that capsized, could you swim to safety with the baby on your chest? And so on.

The worst part, you realize as you gaze at the oblivious baby, is that it won't care if you tow it to safety and expire in the attempt, if you sacrifice yourself in one final effort to save it from disaster. Most likely later will look back and wonder, not at your selfless mother love, but at how you could imperil it in the first place. How come you didn't know. Your failure, again, to predict absolutely everything that could go wrong.

5. Sucks

EVERYBODY NEEDS A HOBBY or consuming passion and the baby discovered its shortly after delivery. One of the books you read, back when you could read, asserted that newborn babies, if given the chance, will crawl up their mothers' bellies and take their first sucks right after birth. Since then it has not stopped eating. You read Freud in a former life, when you had two brain cells to rub together. He explained human development as a movement from passive to active, giving the baby who moves from being suckled to suckling as example. Freud you idiot. In its first moments the baby is already on top, contentedly in charge, while you lie there wondering how your widely dispersed parts will ever meet again.

It's not pleasant to imagine the baby this way, as a leering guy on the corner, but there's no denying its opportunistic nature. Every time you pick it up, coo and chuck, it twists violently in your arms. Mouth open and aimed, no doubt of what it wants. Every time you cradle it in your arms, look lovingly down at its peaceful face, that face opens in a preparatory tremble. Get to it. The baby might as well be the director of a *Moms Gone Wild* video. Come on, bring 'em out, hop to it, let's move, hungry here. Your worst suspicions confirmed: it sees you solely as the repository and purveyor of Thing One and Thing Two.

Among the baby's faults is a deplorably shortsighted selfishness. Even when you explain you have to feed yourself so as to meet its incessant demands it continues to screech and wave its arms. You imagine the message it tries so urgently to convey. *I'm dying.*

Honestly, I'm dying here. My stomach is empty. Empty! This is serious. You don't seem to understand. Put down the spoon. Quit making whatever's in the pot. Piccck me up. I'm starving. That's it, I'm really going to let loose. I'm going to—I'm going to—Oh? Okay. That's better. I—num, num, snorkle, snuff.

There's nothing pretty about the baby's technique. It's like your neighbour's pug dog, truffling for a treat. You would like to explain to the baby, as if it cared, that you are not used to being handled this way. The twin temples deserve a certain reverence, a look of delight, a consciousness of the favour being conferred. It would do well to pause, you inform the hoovering baby, and glance at you in momentary appreciation. Rather than cramming whatever it can reach into its mouth with deplorable greed. You despair of ever teaching the baby manners.

If only your loved ones sympathized. Instead they've realized that a feeding baby at least ceases its otherwise constant complaint. *Maybe it's hungry,* your elder daughter's quick to say, *maybe you should feed it.* You thought she'd be squeamish, tell you to put them away. Hah. Again? It's like being a hooker. Seriously. Roll over, tab A, slot B, think about something else. Maybe read. Why not? The baby doesn't care. If you could detach your breasts, you could leave.

You pick up the morning paper, flip through with your free hand. Stop at the World section. Famine in Ethiopia again, a colour picture of a child malnourished to bone. You turn the page, you can't even look.

6. Just a Cigar

YOUR NEIGHBOUR ARRIVES and hoists the baby in her arms, a butcher weighing a roast. In the days and weeks after its birth the baby is no more than a wrapped bundle: cased sausage, rolled cigar, swathed missile. The dog, uncaring, noses at her feet.

One day the baby wakes. Its hand, rising above the swaddle, hails atremble: yoo hoo. It emits a noise: interrogative, inquiring. The dog at once aquiver, all attention, stands on its hind legs to peer at the astonishing transformation. What have we here, what is this object?

Dogs are perplexed by babies. They are human but unlike, so staggery and erratic. Their size an additional mystery, so much less than a person should be. Their helplessness obvious, so that the dog must protect them even at hazard to itself: their feeble grab and grip, unpredictable falls and flings. And the noises they make, free of the familiar cadences of speech. *What is this, what is it doing here, where has it come from, when will it go?* You understand the dog's point, sympathize even. Sometimes you wonder the same things yourself.

7. My Sentence

THE BABY WAKES in the middle of the night screaming. You dimly remember feeding it earlier, and your resolution not to let it suckle if it woke again: *can't keep getting up like this, need my sleep, not a vending machine,* etcetera. Like a longstanding grudge, your reasoning eludes you. Only the spent conviction remains.

The baby screams, and screams, and screams. You've figured out that it likes to lie on its front and suck its fingers to soothe itself to sleep. But of course when you flip the baby onto its face (none too gently you must admit) it twists around and lies there, mouth open, emitting a truly awful noise.

Call the authorities.

There's an emergency, come quick. I can't get any sleep. Take this thing away.

If it was a fire alarm, you'd remove the batteries. A party, the police would be at the door. A toy, you'd sue the manufacturer. A concert, you'd get up and walk out. Hellish, earsplitting, rambunctious, hitting every part of the spectrum from on high to reverberating bass, the baby is truly a wonder, if only one could put it under glass and charge admission. Punch in your credit card number to hear the earsplitting screams. Watch the mouth widen. Marvel at how it never stops.

So of course you and your loved one begin to argue.

When did you last feed her?

I don't remember.

You're lying by the clock and you didn't happen to notice?

You didn't open your eyes?

What about you? you counterattack, diverting. *What are you doing over there?*

With the lake of baby between you, lake of screams.

Why shouldn't I be over here? Besides, you told me to come over here.

No I didn't. Now you're arguing about things of which you have no actual knowledge, having been consigned to oblivion at the time. Maybe you did tell him to go over there, maybe you did capriciously refuse to feed the baby, maybe you only dreamed that she fed once in the night already. And still the scream goes on, just varied enough that one can't really tune it out, although you proceed to accuse him of just that. *You were snoring.*

I wasn't snoring. Another illogical denial, his turn now, given that one can't be awake to hear oneself, but you let it pass; you've plenty of stockpiled ammunition. It's hard to hear the words of invective with the squall in the middle of the bed.

I'd like to just leave.

What?

I said I'd like to leave.

Go ahead. Go home. Finally, exasperated, he picks up the baby, who stops its horrendous howl at once, even manages to smile at you over his shoulder, like the opportunist it is. *What are you doing?* he demands, as you get up to follow.

I'm coming with you.

Why?

To make sure you don't feed the baby. There's breastmilk in the freezer: he doesn't make it, so he doesn't understand how precious it is. He's a surprisingly passionate advocate of feeding on demand. Food, his answer to everything. *Maybe it's hungry*, he'll say, *maybe you should feed it.*

Why shouldn't I feed the baby? he says, now.

It's your stance, on the other hand, that with milk given each time it yowls the baby will continue to wake up throughout the night, disrupting everyone's sleep but especially yours. Only the granite lesson of absence, its learning not to depend on you, will mitigate its unreasonable want.

So it'll learn to get back to sleep without me.

When the baby was first born you both minded your manners more; you were helpless and he solicitous. Now you've got some of your strength back and with it the energy for these arguments, ones that you partially realize are about nothing more than the unbearable fact of being trapped, baby's hostage, no alternative but to lie there and take it. With your last spark, though, you'll show him. See just how awful I can be.

8. You Heard

THERE ARE TIMES when the baby's beastly nature is in abeyance. When the baby's head falls oh so sweetly onto your breastbone and, swaying heavily, settles there. Times that only occur, big surprise, when the baby is asleep.

You attend a performance in a small café, praying all the while. Please let her sleep and not scream, please let nobody look and frown, please don't make the author stop reading aloud, lean down and ask you to leave like that other time. You strap the baby, yowling in protest, to your front. Moments pass, silence: you risk a look. She has sweetly and simply tumbled aslumber. The poet finishes. Just in time you jam your fingers into baby's ears. You know from experience how applause shakes them, the timbre of it. When they tested baby's newborn hearing you were foolish enough to take pride when they said:

Best on the ward.

They use a probe, deliver a chime, measure the response of the tiny hairs that line the canal. Non-invasive, they can even do it when the baby's asleep.

The things you do to placate baby, all the while swearing you won't let baby run you:

How you freeze once baby's asleep, not daring to move no matter how uncomfortable your position, lest your movement wake her;

The increasing amount of gack you take with you wherever you go, boiled water in a bottle to stave off its inevitable demand for milk, approved educational toy for it to ignore, diaper, tote bag, another diaper, plastic bag for diapers, cloth in case it goes everywhere, blanket in case it ever sleeps again, nursery sink;

The places you won't go after baby's bedtime, God forbid it should be cranky, and when you do, those rare occasions, it's as if you're avoiding natural disaster when no screeching meltdown occurs, whew, dodged that bullet.

And the excuses you make for it, he and you both.

Maybe it's teething (this for months);

Maybe it had a bad dream (when it wakes up screaming);

Maybe it's too early;

Too late;

Too hot;

Too cold;

Slept too much;

Didn't sleep enough;

It's hungry;

It has indigestion;

Diarrhea;

Constipation;

Too much, too little, too big, too small, too soon, too late, too long, too short. Everything must be done for it before it thinks to complain, everything right and nothing wrong. Don't rouse it, don't rile it, don't annoy it: you'll be sorry if you do.

And now the voice of the eternal critic chimes in: *you monsters, bathing it in water that warm, putting off the feed for your own selfish reasons, letting it lie face-down on the carpet even if it didn't complain at the time: what were you thinking? How is the baby supposed to tell you? Who are the adults in this picture?*

Anything rather than face the truth.

There is no right answer, never was, and never will be.

9. Doomed

YOU IMAGINED THAT WHEN THE BABY began to grow, when it could at last master its own eyes and fingers (focus, grasp objects, compose letters to the United Nations protesting its maltreatment) that you might finally get some peace. But when you unwisely place its bucket seat by the desk in an attempt to catch up on three hundred unread emails, the baby seizes the chance to indulge its newfound passion for paper.

Elsewhere, life continues. Unsolicited emails beseeching you to complete lengthy online surveys, links to interesting articles you don't have time to read, and invites you'll ignore as ever, to magazine launch parties held in hip nightclubs or costly but fun fundraising dinners, but now you get to blame the baby. Then the end-of-term pleas, from students who've been AWOL all semester, to raise their marks or they'll die. Meanwhile, the overflow from the haphazardly piled correspondence you swore you'd tidy centuries ago sifts floorward. Unticked baby-proofing checklists with their dire warnings, your implacably mounting sperm-bank balance, the shining prospectuses of private schools where you plan to send the baby as early as practicable. Alerted by the unusual silence, you look down. The baby is masticating gently, savouring the textures of cardboard and gloss. When you pry the wads of gooey pulp out of its mouth the baby reacts with predictable outrage, screaming as if you're attempting to remove its appendix on the battlefield, sans anesthetic.

In what you already foresee will be a doomed attempt to

distract baby, you place it facedown on its mat. Bedecked with soft patterned shapes, padded plastic mirrors, and attached squeezy toys, this approved activity centre has so far found no favour with the tiny despot, you suspect because nothing on offer holds out the alluring possibility of immediate demise.

Still, you give it the old nursery try. *Look,* you say, on the desperate rising tone of unsuccessful activity directors every-where, *tummy time! Ooh, this button makes a chicken noise! Here, dog!* You squeeze, explanatory, and produce a faraway howl. The baby regards you blankly.

The baby's only saving grace is its stupidity. It can amuse itself merely by staring at its fingers (*what? how did these get here?*). It likes to chew on stray bits of whatever outfit you've decided to stuff it into that day since, due no doubt to its in-cessant feeding, it can barely fit into clothes designed for babies three months older. Mostly it reclines Roman fashion, all that's missing a couch and some grapes, although you have an idea who's been cast in the thankless role of enslaved attendant. Negligently it examines a ribbon of paper you've somehow overlooked, despite sweeping pretty much daily, on account of the probably flaking hundred-year-old lead paint. Gulps it down before you can intervene. Oh well. Fibre.

Dear Sirs. Thank you for your communication of the 21st instant. Enclosed please find payment for services rendered. Please excuse the appearance of the return stub, as it has been gummed by an infant. I remain, dear Sirs, your most obedient servant. Anyone but the baby's. Oh please.

10. Only a Fool Would

WHAT ARE YOU DOING?

What?

I said what are you doing?

I'm cleaning it. We do that.

Using that soap? Are you mad?

You think you have already established that the baby is, to put it mildly, not delicate. That it can take or break with the best of them. Yet your loved one insists you use its special baby soap to clean its crevices and folds (and, oh Lord, there are so many of them). How dare he? And then you realize: just like you and your older daughter, he believes he knows the baby best.

What makes you all observe the baby so closely? Everyone's noticed how the noise of the vacuum cleaner elicits agonized screams. Its favourite positions are a map you've learnt by heart. Your older daughter has figured out how to make it chuckle wetly by faking a sprawling pratfall across the back of the couch. You'd imagine she gave you a head start on this motherhood business, this girl of yours, indubitably still alive at nine, but the fact is that of her babyhood you remember only the big highs and lows. Putting her in the middle of your Easter table, carseat and all. The swing that unpredictably did or didn't soothe. Five a.m. despair.

11. Good Lookin'

THERE COMES A POINT when you and your loved one both confess: you're enchanted by, enamoured of, absolutely enraptured with baby.

The baby itself is as fat and unbecoming as ever. One night you feel a sensation like someone is rolling your nipple between finger and thumb. Waking to find out who could be perpetrating this outrage, this assault, you discover it cosily sucking away. Somehow you forgot to turn on the electric fence, secure the portcullis in the closed position, and even in its sleep the baby knew enough to take advantage.

Its personality has not improved; nay, more the reverse. It pulls your hair in a vain attempt to lever itself upright, twists its fingers in your skin as if crumpling a tissue, closes a gummy fist on the glasses you've just cleaned, again, sticks its fingers up your loved one's nose if given the chance, and even toothless tries to bite.

As human beings go, it is an unprepossessing specimen. Its legs are frankly obese, with folds you have previously seen only in American supermarkets. Its head is a giant bobble. It already has a paunch, and it jiggles. The whole of it seems to sag, as if irresistibly pulled by gravity; even its genital area bulges like something about to spill over. But when you speak to it now, it gives you a sly little smile, and when it sees its own image in the mirror it grins with a fantastic delight.

But its best trick, the one that really drives you crazy, is how it acts when you come back. Jumping up and down in your loved one's arms, crowing, flapping its own arms and generally expressing its great pleasure in being yours, claimed again.

12. Go Away

THE BABY KICKS AND TWISTS while you lie there moaning. Make it stop, make it go to sleep, make it be quiet however; you don't care anymore. But no, you have responsibilities. You must ensure it doesn't stuff its head into the crack between bed and frame and snap its neck, fling itself face first six inches to the floor, or inhale the pillow and suffocate.

If the baby would only go into a basket, a nice handwoven one to show you cared, that you could lower out the window. And then if only some kindly soul on the floor beneath would discover it, take it in and deal with it.

If somehow you could be relieved at a stroke of the baby's incessant presence, its demands that you look, pay attention, interact, notice meeee.

If only.

You have no desire to kill the baby. That would imply an active role in the process. It's simply that yesterday, when the baby went for its shots, the doctor took the opportunity to stick you with a purportedly innocuous vaccine. Now your whole body aches, each joint telegraphing its exact painful position. You know the only answer to your suffering is a temporary oblivion. But who can be oblivious with the tewwible babby demanding your attentions?

The terrible baby has begun to scream. It screams until you lift it into your lap, where it puts its head back. What it wants. What it always wants.

13. Sainted

TODAY YOUR LOVED ONE calls your attention from the screen in disgust: *look at this.* Propped in its seat, papers somehow again within reach, the baby gums his chequebook wetly. *Can you not keep better track of these things?* Splashing the gasoline, lighting the match: whoosh of leaping flame.

Can you not understand that I can barely do two things at once, you snap, above the sudden roar of the bushfire in your head. *Let's look at how much time you've had to work this week, shall we?* This despite the fact that he has cooked you not one meal but two, has cheerfully run the terrible vacuum, ignoring the attendant screams, has cleaned the filthy baby after its grunting exertions, ew, has brought you tea in bed that very morning, tea and a newspaper and a grapefruit he sectioned himself, the darling. Is generally far better than you who lie there moaning, who beg for one extra minute of sleep. Please God, whatever you want, take it on credit, foreclose in future, declare me morally bankrupt in years to come, I just don't care.

He reminds you that he would have been watching the baby himself but for cleaning after the meal he cooked and served. *So?* you interrupt. *So?* Although just remembering the hash browns—browned and crisp, the plate an object of beauty, bacon fat and meaty, eggs over easy, plenty of pulp in the orange juice. *I'm gaining weight again, better not eat too much,* you said, and then winked and ordered this menu. Ordered! What do you have to complain about, exactly?

24

In the middle of the night for the first time your loved one makes the baby a bed on the floor in the other room. Then you both decide that room is too far away so he moves the baby's little pallet into your room. Then at one o'clock in the morning, when the baby wakes, your loved one decides to bring it back into bed. And despite its terrible habits—the way it pees through one leg of its diaper so that it misses the diaper entirely and soaks the sheet, how it ends up sideways so that you both have to cling to the extreme edges of the bed, the abandon with which it pinches your nose and cheek in its sleep—you are both silently relieved.

14. More Hell

THE BABY LIES ON THE FLOOR CRYING, drumming its legs on the boards. The neighbours. What they must think. The baby has developed new habits. When you push a shirt over its head it begins to scream and thrusts itself violently backwards. You are tempted to let the baby's soft skull fall where it may but once again, despite its best efforts to brain itself, it is your job to thwart its obvious desire for permanent injury.

Last night the baby woke when you arrived home at ten at night. The baby had slept for the sitter, thank goodness. At least now she won't automatically refuse you next time. It had rested well, ready now for the long hours of play ahead. It smiled and opened its eyes wide and treated you to its cheery little grin. Your heart sank, weighted by dismay.

At five the baby was up again. You were surprisingly rested; for once it had slept a solid six hours. Greedy for more, you tried settling it back to sleep by the simple expedient of holding it down. When this didn't work you removed the baby to its pallet. It struggled, crying, and the sobs, the lifelong damage you were no doubt inflicting, weakened your resolve so that you lifted it back into bed. The baby held your arm, still racked by grief. Given its recent trauma, it soothed itself by ripping at your flesh.

You stood the plucking for seconds until, patience once again in shards, you pushed the baby out of arm's reach. This made the baby cry again, so once more you gathered it close, after which it had to soothe itself, which led to it ripping at your flesh, which made you push it away, which made it cry, repeat, repeat, repeat, until you're dead.

15. Friendly Game

WHAT KILLS YOU ABOUT THE BABY, between screams, is its imperturbable good cheer. Listen to the way it lies there babbling to itself, well, to your loved one to be more specific. What exactly is so important for it to communicate?

A ba ba ba ba ba ba ba.

A ba way.

Wa eigh.

And listen to him, cooing back: *Aw.*

Aw wa weigh wa waaaa.

At four in the morning you two attempt what is meant to be a private rendezvous. Ah, the delicious prospect of touching again, you who slept entwined every night pending the terrible baby's arrival. You begin the delicate, doomed process of shifting the warm bundle that bisects the bed. The two of you handle it like unexploded ordinance, shrinking and already braced lest it wake. Which of course it does.

At first it displays its usual cheer—*Hey, great, we're all up!*—but soon enough its mood sours. It demands to be nursed, yet again might you add, and when you attempt to fob it off with one breast screams and jerks and goes into its usual routine. *I'm dying, dying I tell you, starving to death before your very eyes, are you actually going to allow this crime against nature, this outrage to humanity? I'll call the police, I'll alert the authorities, human rights violation, atrocity, ah, that's better, num num, suck.* A routine which, if it ever convinced, certainly doesn't nowadays, given how the baby runneth over.

Crime against nature? Outrage to humanity? Let's list the baby's for a start. How it invariably falls into slumber when you're out walking, far from the mountain of paperwork awaiting your any spare moment. Hope springs, foolish and ever renewable, as it continues unconscious through the worst rattles and shakes of carriage over cobblestones and ruts. You're leaping hillock and fording stream in your haste to get home, where the bare snick of the latch, as you tiptoe with the usual useless infinite delicacy towards bed, brings it instantly to wide-eyed wake. Your fingers already itch for the keyboard, that neglected instrument, for your moldering email inbox; but it is not to be, the tewwible, tewwible babby will see to that.

And then the babby is a Jekyll and Hyde: in daylight and in company all smiles, at night an unmedicated psychiatric patient howling mayhem and riot into your ear, beyond reason, this instant. *Aw, how cute,* say the uninitiated in the elevator, at sight of its happy face. Yes but. You stutter to a stop. Impossible to explain the magnitude of its duplicity. Its lack of sense, moderation, comprehension: your fury. Your needs.

You're barely keeping the pilot light of your interrupted rendezvous lit now. Sure enough, when it finally finishes the world's longest feed, it refuses to go quietly back to sleep, instead pokes its head up anew, surveys your fumbling attempts with interest. *Hey! What are you two doing?* You give up, as always. Baby coming up trumps again, big surprise.

16. Emergency Response

YOU STRIP THE BABY'S DIAPER OFF, its morning change shamefully postponed, only to find the half-suspected punchline, wet yellow semicolon, ha ha, colon, that's good, or will be when you can laugh about this, let's say two or three millennia down the road.

You wrinkle your nose, wondering idly about the smell: particular, or universal? During gestation you moved to Japan with your loved one, where he had a temporary position. For the first time the flavours of okonomiyaki, takoyaki, and udon struck you as noxious. As a palliative you took your growing belly down a long skinny street where you found a restaurant that served minute portions of highly flavoured curries, precise molded pats of cooked rice, giant naan. While you ate you watched the television: video after video of coy maidens and gallant suitors singing and dancing on rural hillsides. Did those meals and that music become a part of baby, imprinted, inhabit it, to be expelled all these months later, in this exclamatory squiggle?

You hook its bird-bone ankles, your own hips canted back, and swipe the cloth at its cheeks. The squalling intensifies. *Help, I'm dying, she's killing me, she's cutting off my leg, aggh, there goes my internal organ, I haven't learned them yet so I'm not sure which one, argh, argh, call the authorities, emergency, outrage, maltreatment.*

Ah, the basic unfairness of it all, that it's baby who can scream and cry, flail and thrash, attempt to escape. You thought you got away, didn't you, from your own country and its strictures, for that time in Japan at least. You left your world behind, and it didn't make a damned bit of difference. You're still required to display the exact same tolerance, care, even devotion, in the face of this exact disgusting production, effluvia, stinking mess. What's fair about that? Why can't you be the one to run screaming into the street, book a ticket back to the land of teppanyaki this minute, at the very least toss your head and howl like the barnyard dog button Velcroed to baby's utterly ignored activity centre?

17. Proof

THE BABY HAS LEARNED an unpleasant new skill which, as per the programming of its robot masters, it must practice incessantly. Unfortunately the masters forgot to program in an elementary discrimination. The searing front of your Modern Maid gas oven, piping unguarded radiators, bowls brimful of just-simmered soup: the baby burns to touch them all. *Hot!* you say in warning, yanking the baby back. Oblivious to hazard, it continues to stretch yearning, tiny fingers. Admit it: you might as well instruct a loaf of bread.

You subside, cease your sluggish efforts, shrug, roll your eyes. Who can fix it, who can predict everything, who has the time to cage faucets, insulate cocoa, buy spill-proof cups? You'll take baby's chances. Nature's course, or as your neighbour observed, could be you're just lazy.

18. Dry

WHEN YOU FIND YOURSELF IN COMPANY with other addicts, it's the one thing you discuss. Dispense with the preliminaries. Barely introduce yourselves, bother learning the babies' names: how cute, who cares. What really matters: *how long?*

Oh, seven hours, say the other mothers. *Through the night. Soon as he was born. Yes,* they smile, *we're lucky.* You stare through narrowed, gritty eyes. *They're lying. Must be lying.* But what's left of your brain insists on arguing. *Why? Why would they taunt you? How about you,* say the mothers, kindly, *how's she?*

Oh, she's up twice, you say, *twice a night.* See, you don't count the feed at her bedtime, nobody counts that one. Or the time when you go to bed, when she wakes and seeks you. Or in the morning, early in the morning, well five, practically morning anyhow, then seven, you're lucky she even sleeps to seven, so better not count that one either. But they're still watching you with pity, still sorry for you, and you can't stand it.

What you don't tell them that they can see anyway: how the baby has worn you to a nub, used your breasts until they are the texture of old flannel, much washed. How the baby goes back for more, again and again, even when they're empty, even when you have nothing left. *Can't you tell,* you whisper to its bent head, *don't you get it?* The baby oblivious, sucking away.

How you resent the baby's unrelenting hunger, its refusal to pace itself. No husbanding of supplies here, no looking to future generations. You're its ever-renewable resource. Peak milk? Please. You don't mention your daily prayer. *Give it up, take it away, begone: anything, just let me rest.* You refrain from explaining how your loved one enters the room as if in answer. Silently picks up the baby. They leave, practically floating. How, left, you sink, and the dark closes over. Another hour of sleep. Time written off, lead apron draped over your midsection, a continental shelf of slumber to fall over in slow motion, drifting to the sea floor far below. You say nothing of this.

You forbear to describe how, roused at last by faraway complaint, you call drowsily. Your loved one comes, hands you the baby. Rolled flat with sleep, warm in the bed, you fold it into your front. The baby's whole length presses against you, pinchy wet fingers to the cold feet it seems not to notice or mind, as it searches out a breast. For once you glimpse baby's point of view. How delicious, to nestle in your arms, unfurl against your warmth, root for your chest. How perfect, to be loved like this. You don't tell them any of this. You're sure they know it all anyway.

19. Evergreen

BATTLE PITCHED, LINES DRAWN, baby with a devil in its hand: devil ornament, that your daughter hung incautiously from the bottom branch of the tree.

Christmas is coming, with its brightly wrapped tributes. Your older daughter favours a toy system of small parts: teeny swords and flowers and kittens, small cylindrical labelled cans and bottles, tinier teddy bears for tiny babies put to sleep in plastic cribs with moulded blankets and minute hanging mobiles that actually turn. Each morning and evening your daughter attends to their myriad relationships: the marriages, the brothers, the children, the mothers. She gives them all meals, puts them to bed. Would that it were so easy. Christmas morning will be a further onslaught, yacht and desert fort playsets snarled in a litter of paper, tinsel and plastic discarded in corners. Lord grant the day won't end in the emergency room, your standard waking nightmare, with the tewwible babby being plumbed.

Now the infant in question, innocent of its potential fate, examines with great interest a papier-maché heart bearing an image of a sickly-looking angel. Yanks it from its branch. You could swear the baby cannot move so far, but for the evidence in its hand. The phone rings.

Hello, are you interested in supporting family-friendly enter-tainment in Canada? reads the lady in a sing-song. *Hollywood won't support movies that don't have profanity, nudity and violence because they think they're too soft. You can support us by ordering two of our movies for only $19.99.*

You say no, no chance to add before the lady rings off that you are all for nudity and profanity, movie violence your only possibility of excitement, relief from the numb real world. *Send me your violent movies, profanity lady, let me watch and rate 'em. Bring me back to a world without babies: strapped bicep, hefted belt, potty mouth, great guns.* You glance back at baby. The devil is gone: successfully swallowed, discarded elsewhere? Baby's face neutral, clueless, now or ever.

20. Warning Notice

THIS YEAR THE HOSPITAL PRODUCED A DVD it sent home with every new mother, including you. Topic: *don't shake the baby*. You don't watch it: who doesn't know already, who has time?

When you leave the house, though, you remind the sitter: *don't shake the baby*.

And she solemnly reiterates: *I won't shake the baby*.

Don't bludgeon the baby, you add.

Don't set the baby on fire.

Whatever you do, do not drop the baby out the window.

The baby must not be harmed in any way. Harms include contusion, concussion, intubation, palpitations, or other aberrations, sensations, or classifications. The baby should not be suppurating. You will be most displeased should the baby return with, for instance, a sucking chest wound. Do not attempt to mitigate any dereliction in duty by, say, dropping the baby off at another caregiver's and absconding, leaving it to sink into unconsciousness. The baby must be perfect when you return, as it would be under your own care.

Hah.

Earlier today the baby retched and out came a penny, freshly shone.

Later the baby hurled again and deposited, among the contents of its stomach, a smiley-face sticker from a strip of them you'd unwisely allowed it to hold. The sticker still unsmirched, metallic, indigestible.

You weave home after two cocktails. Now, the baby insists.

Now. You sigh and give in. Alcohol's effects on development, lead's slow accretion in the tissues, Christmas lights to shatter or short, hazards every one. Season's greetings, ho ho ho.

21. Brown Study

YOU GO TO THE CHILDREN'S AREA at the library. Can you, might you persuade the tewwible babby to play by itself so that you can work for once? Should this unlikely plan succeed you must disembowel yourself straddling one of the punitive child-size seats, ignore the tears of youngsters awaiting the computers reserved for their use, swear not to access any sites promoting family-friendly entertainment in Canada, with their graphic examples of what not to watch. You'll do it and gladly. Whichever kidney they need, however deaf you'll need to be to the sharply indrawn breath of librarians, how blinkered to ignore the signs warning of death and worse should you leave your child unattended.

Amongst the puppets and puzzles you sight a mother who makes you want to weep. Is it her outfit, perfect jeans, perfect beaten-in brown leather belt, is it her clean-lined, hawk-nosed face, is it her air of imperturbable good humour with two children under five? At first you thought she must be a nanny, she was so young and hip and she actually played with the children, not like you; the only excuse must be that she was getting paid.

You end up having to watch the tewwible babby the whole time. Fascinated by older children, it ignores the soft giant blocks and pegboards reserved for infants, instead seizing the opportunity to wrap its fingers solidly about their wire puzzles. The children give their mothers supplicating looks, only to be met with unhelpful admonitions (*Careful! It's a baby!*).

So you do your best to pry off the infant armoured vehicle, with it of course screaming all the while in outrage. Its future as a protester assured.

The baby likes the other mother too. As she passes it looks up at her and clutches her leg. *Take me home,* you both beg her silently. *Rescue me. I'm the hostage, the victim here: can't you see, don't you know what she's doing to me?*

22. Prospectus

THE BABY HAS ATTAINED a new and terrible ability. Now it can crawl. For weeks you've been arguing that it wasn't actually crawling, because (crucial element here) *its back legs weren't moving.* This very morning you watched one leg, then the other, the clockwork patterning of them. No denying it: the emotion you felt was fear.

When you put the baby to bed now it rights itself, glances around with a look of naked delight (*see how clever I am!*) and resists your concerted suggestions, some not so polite, that it friggin' go to sleep.

Your loved one lies down beside the baby and closes his eyes. Centuries pass, a stone age accretes. Glaciers solidify, tower, lurch finally into movement. At last the baby timbers face first to the bed. When your loved one reappears among the living, he's pallid and bloodless, leached by effort. Putting the baby to sleep is not easy.

When the baby wakes in the morning it sits up and at once dives headfirst for the edge of the bed, stopped only by your almost automatic hand. Face it. The baby has no concept of how past results guarantee future performance. The baby is no mutual fund but an independent concern.

And there's you, its mainstay and life raft. Who'll get blamed when things go wrong? The baby? Hardly. Will anyone commiserate? Of course not. They'll simply ask, in that tone they use, what you were doing when the baby fell out the window.

Satisfying the courier.

Oh.

You might as well have been plugging its dangerous bottles, anchoring the diapers, boiling furniture. No matter. One squish, one break, one piece of impermeable Mylar caught in its gullet and all eyes turn to the source of the catastrophe, the fount of the damage: The Mother. Even if it wasn't your balloon. Even if you're the one who'll have to live with the brain damage.

It makes you sick, just thinking about it.

By the age of six months the baby should be able to, says the incredibly annoying baby book, dented anew from where you've thrown it against the wall. Again. Pick up a Cheerio, smile, wave, turn at the sound of its name. Who cares. What you really want to know: when it can dress itself, pack its own bags, be entertained by strangers while you snake away to do ... what?

All babies are different, says the book. If your baby has not attained these developmental milestones it may not necessarily be stunted. It could simply be lagging, not so bad in the context of war, forced migration, or drought. Your doctor is a trained professional. Call her for help in accepting the inevitable: its any problem, your fault.

23. Free Advice

THE BABY IS STUPENDOUS. Its legs bulging pillars. Its head enormous. Folds in the plump skin of its forearms. Its feet and hands dainty by comparison. No surprise really; like a tick it's maintained a newborn feeding schedule, every two hours for the past six months. Falling off only when bloated, burping loudly.

You consult on when to start the giant on solids. *You have to feed it by spoon*, interrupts the doctor, unasked. *Babies this age are inefficient.* You opine as to how it could afford to lose a little weight and the doctor fixes you with a look. *Don't be fat-phobic.*

You should take better care of the baby, your loved one says sternly. You know what he means. No more sitting at your desk staring at the screen while it explores the sister's litter of China-crafted toy parts, fashioned no doubt from recycled computer components and used plutonium. No more trading off its interested excavations of the wastepaper basket, with the tasty cargo of spent hair and used tissues, for a few more minutes of work. The baby must be penned and controlled, allowed only whittled European playthings daubed with vegetable-based paint ($29.95 each). No use protesting that it entirely ignores its big box of toys, occupies itself instead strewing the contents of your storage basket about the room: fur hats, clutch purses, white gloves. Ah, pretensions.

24. The Plot

WHAT KIND OF SEA MONSTER is the baby? An octopus, wrapping myriad limbs around yours in the dark, fashioning its mouth into a carp-like O? When the four of you arrive at the resort for the weekend you order a crib at once. It arrives, a small rolling box of iron bars, the lion's cage in a circus picture. Giddy with relief, you vow that tonight, at least, the baby will not twine about you, suck you under. Bedtime comes. The baby twists in its small prison, clutching the bars with miniature fists. From your bathroom perch you are treated to the sight of its hectic cheeks and streaming eyes. Complaint assails your ears. Where does the baby learn to inspire such pity, where do they all?

Perhaps the baby does not come from the sea, amniotic, but from the dense cities where it was bred. In that case it must be a miniature godzilla or king kong, scattering the playmobil city with its giant limbs if only the sister would allow it into her room. But no, you have explained in detail what will happen, painting in gruesome colours the trip to the emergency room to disgorge the tiny sword or tinier cap, or even worse the weary wait for it to emerge naturally. So at home the sister keeps closed the door upon which the baby pushes, resists its will.

The baby could be a creature of plain or savanna, a young impala just finding its shaky limbs. This explains why it must drag itself from room to room, one limb useless behind, heedless of doors and hallways and stairs and roads. Or perhaps the baby was maimed when the monsters without warning attacked.

Is it one of them, or must it be protected? This is the dilemma of the humans left behind, as they hesitate with pitchforks & burning brands. *Do we repel or welcome, are you to be rescued or destroyed?*

25. Ring the Circle

THE BABY WAKES IN THE MORNING your sunshine, yours and his both, and O you laugh together with sheer delight at the sight of its rosy peach cheeks, its round moon of a head balanced absurdly on the miniature clown body. The baby is a cherub, tubby and adored, a small glowing sun rotating with all the force of its warmth upon you. You open to it in your turn and then to each other, smiling and smiling. The payoff, the motherlode, the prize. What needs daylight, clear skies, or even summer, when you can bask in these rays?

Now the baby's ball of light fragments and breaks, one trembling piece left there on the wall, as fresh conquests beckon. Tipping glasses to spin sideways, precariously edged. Now the baby bowls over the stroller and, jarred, finds itself in a pickle, howling for help. Now it has four buck teeth, sticking out top and bottom: now its grin splits cheeks. Now the baby stands shining again beside the bath, flips the handle for the faucet. Off. On. Off. On. Offon. Onnnnn. Offonoffonoffff. You know what this is about, you're no fool. The baby cares little for your adoration, seeks only mastery. 23,000 genes, some shared with fish. Its mouth turns to you, open, O, in wonder.

26. Racked, Shelf, Nice Pair of Teeth

WHEN YOU GET BACK HOME the baby sitting in his lap is happy enough to see you but something's different. Seven hours you've been gone, and the baby doesn't try to reel you in, isn't waving its arms to guide the big plane to the gate. You bare your breast, ripening now, lavish. You could have sworn that every man in the bus on the way here registered you, exact, where you were sitting and the dimensions of your rapidly swelling bosom. But baby isn't impressed. It sucks politely for a few minutes, drawing off the top milk, looking around. Clearly wanting to be elsewhere.

I think you could wean, he says.

Wean? Wean from these horrible nights, this recurring dishevelment, your hostage status? Wean from the pluck of its cries, the threat behind its nighttime stirrings, the knowledge that if you don't give it the two things it wants you'll be sorry? Have you grown so weary of the tell-tale blooms slowly exploding on your blouses, the post-natal drip of the forsaken twin awaiting its turn? *It's too early,* you say, *the books say not for a year,* and that whole day and night you go to it gladly. Your staggered breaths rise and entwine, as you clutch it close. Wordless, elemental, evolving: gush and suck and swallow, the beat of its small hurry heart against your stronger slow one, its eyes unfocused as it takes the hit, dissolves in pleasure. What else do you have, if not this?

27. Columbus Junior

TODAY YOU ARGUE ABOUT FOOD. First exhibit Doctor Spock, circa 1932. Egg yolks and meat at two months, well, skip that, but here, evidence:

Vegetables are commonly added to a baby's diet at–

Strained and boiled, interrupts your loved one. A man who totes baby cereal in a cup, who has bananas on his counter but feeds bananas from a jar, who never met an instant food he didn't like. Rash-inducing citrus fruit, whole or processed grains, the suitability of ground-up adult meals, individually or in a mess, ages one can chew, appropriate finger foods: each of you marshal these arcane details in service to your diametrically opposed points of view. It is his contention that on your regimen of cooked beans and raw vegetables the baby wakes at night over and over, screaming in pain as it attempts to digest the unpalatable lumps. It is yours that to feed it instant food and give it water from a bottle is to fatally nip its budding desire to chew, suck, and gnaw on foods of differing textures, colours, and tastes. You recognize that these galvanized positions could meet somewhere in the middle, and you comfort yourself with the knowledge that on a diet of alternating whole foods and mush the baby is probably getting all it needs, that and you.

The argument dries up over dinner, as it takes its first bites of spaghetti noodles. Sucking them in one side of its mouth, plucking them out the other with delicate fingers. Barely breathing, you both watch. Little epicure, new world.

28. All Night (Refrain)

THE BABY WAKES AND WAKES AND WAKES. God knows how tired you are of these nights broken by her cries, how she snorfles and opens her mouth, how even in the dark her glittering eyes turn to you. Yesterday you went to a movie by yourself for the first time since your joint birth. Being alone doesn't feel wrong exactly, but there is a nagging sense of missing: errand undone, thing you forgot to bring, phone call you didn't make. Then you remember, as you shoulder through the throng. The mild shock, as bodies break against your front. Wave of bone and flesh. *Hey watch it. I've got a–* And then the realization: oh no, not tonight.

You miss your loved one. His attention, particularly. You'd like to go to the movies together, talk about the plot afterwards. You tell him what happened but it's not the same. None of the force of it can be conveyed, or the nuances of character. You describe the leading lady's breasts but, again, they really have to be seen to be appreciated. Her superb dress. You'll have to get some superb dresses, have to stop using the baby as an excuse. *I'm tired,* you tell your girlfriend on the phone. *You're always tired,* she says.

Next morning you lie in bed, eyes open, sleep elusive. You remember how it was with your older daughter, the savagery of your desire to be away from her, to have her sleep, to sleep yourself. You remember the desperation, a long-ago, faraway thing, muted now, with this second one.

It's no mystery what you should do, to fix everything. The

schedule, the measured naps, the scientific bedtime. But tomorrow beckons, haphazard, random in its promise, another chance to postpone the sensible. Your plan is different: meandering and squandering. Try that new café, investigate the lunch special, see what's on offer. Always erratic, never a regular.

You catch sight of the baby's face, arriving at the stroller: a wan moon of forlorn. You bend to it and it begins to wave its arms and legs, little kicks, semaphore, yoo-hoo, over here, as if you might overlook it otherwise. *Pick me up, take me, cleave, make us one.* Not so obsolete as you thought, then.

29. Indictment

WHEN VERY DISTRACTED, the baby bites your breast, causing you to scream so loudly everyone in the restaurant looks your way, then quickly away.

Yanks your hair in order to keep its balance. Pulls so hard you discover strands twined in its fingers later, the brute.

When it wakes from sleep, will not calm unless you carry it; and if, as often happens, you have something else to do and must put it down, begins to scream as if its world is ending, apocalypse at the door, and all because you want to put away the dishes.

Wakes up again and again in the night, and will not be consoled unless you feed it over and over, no matter whether you're tired of it, or just tired, sleep pulling you back, or even worse tossing you high and dry, spent on the shingle.

Commences to explore gravity. Hand like a crane, turn and drop, jettisoning the remains of lunch over the side. Expression perfectly blank: *just doin' my job, ma'am*. While you seethe on the seat opposite, your voice rising: No. No. No.

Drags itself up, bangs the headboard, coos and smiles, eats the chips of paint it dislodges with great relish, falls headfirst onto the floor and cries and cries as if you could have stopped it, as if you should have. Which is true, as always.

30. Radiate

THE BABY GLOWS FROM WITHIN, lit by mysterious life. Its cheeks lanterns, its forehead a furnace. Where the doctor with black bag and serious expression, the nurse with instruments ready to hand? Where the wet blankets, the desperate medication? The two of you hover, poor substitutes. You extend yourself, breast to its mouth. It lies there piteously, your flesh for once useless: too weak to feed.

The world presses against the door, a fat man's ooze sealing up the light. Decisions to be made: retrench or relocate, pay up or protest, open hand or closed fist, above board or leave by night? You sleep. Night brings its postscript, cargo of wakefulness. Eyes open, face in the pillow, small flushed bundle of baby slumbering beside.

Morning comes, grainy and leached of colour. A shaky hand-held, student film, too much verité. Your skin sandpaper, your body sacked. Now it's the baby's nap that's fled. It howls and screams from the room where you have barricaded it. Your weak apology on the phone to the office. You move baby to your bed, where despite the light and noise it falls asleep at last still sitting up, fingers jammed in its mouth. Now will sleep past the time you have to leave, now will only reluctantly resume consciousness, now will be a sleepy reproach, echoed by the eternal critic: *you monster, why would you do this to a baby? A sick child.* Your ex-mother-in-law had a rule: for a full day and night after it broke a child with a fever was not allowed outside. How, with four children and no car and nobody else at home? You can't even do it now, sedan at your doorstep, older daughter to get to school, car seat, carrier, trailer, stroller, all mod cons, all the rigmarole, all the supposedly better.

31. The Toll

THE SICKNESS CREEPING UP the back of your throat, baby's sneeze-spread gift from where you leant closer, selfless for once, a Madonna;

The violent colouring around your eyes when you remove your glasses, squint into the mirror: purple, yellow, deep shaded indigo rising to palest pearl, sock it;

Surfacing from sleep (not enough, hardly ever enough) stiff-backed, with hunched shoulders;

Performing your toilette a multiple-choice quiz. Choose one: brush hair, brush teeth, go to bathroom alone, pick outfit deliberately rather than at random, apply lipstick;

The cusp of middle age, the long slow fall. Does the baby bestow youth, or leach it? Who knows, who'll ever know? That one tumbled hair among its fellows: silver, or gold? The catch at the top of your throat where you turn your head, the sag of skin you can locate if you look, which you don't: who needs it, who's got the leisure? How much baby's fault, how much march: month of her birth, passage of time.

32. Runneth

THE MONSTER HAS ACQUIRED NEW SKILLS. It drags itself about the bed like a landed mermaid, more graceful than you'd think. The trouble is that now you are the monster's graveyard buffet, haunted house smorgasbord, city of raisins to squish underfoot.

Ma-ma. It sits up, edges towards you. Pins on its best smile. Instant weight loss, love you forever, make money working from home. You pull the quilt to your chest, tuck it round. *Ma-ma.* Delicate fingers pluck at the coverlet, twitch it away. *Oooh, look. For me?*

Maybe your loved one was right, a thought you consider and immediately dismiss: you could wean. Your breasts are sad, there's no other word for it. They droop and you sympathize. God, we're exhausted. Give us peace. How many times, O Lord, must we rise to the mouth, let go the fluid, make yet more. The elixir the baby takes in greedy swallows, as if abundance came without effort: manna, before the fall, promised land. The baby must suck for minutes before the milk comes down in a gush. After gulping it down there's a lull, a second smaller splash succeeding its later attempts. You rarely let it get to second base, push it away, rearrange your clothes. *There now. You've had your fun, you're satisfied, close enough. Now leave me alone, that's all I ask.* Afterwards, if you're lucky, it'll sleep. On the seventh day, She rested. How you live for its naps, lust for them, those promised minutes of inattention to its every exhaustive need. Buttoning your shirt, mussed. Only to sight a last translucent drop. White stain. Before it's clipped, smothered, soaked, and gone.

33. What We Take From One Another

ASLEEP, BABY THRASHES ABOUT in search of you, smell and weight and sound, you suppose, of your rumbling belly and thumping heart. From your seat in the next room, where you rose when your own slumbers fled, you can hear it toss. It murmurs and chuckles to itself and gives a little cry and you swell foolishly. The baby cannot do without you.

And indeed it quiets only on your return, stills when you speak to it:

knows your voice, thread of reassurance, pulling it forward into its growing.

The baby wakes, open arms. You turn, eager as a lover. Then get it: the forehead slap, d'uh, the fall, the football held for you to kick. The baby has seen no further than the twins, seeks no more than the tap. As ever.

Early morning, awake again, taking the breast, sucking itself back to sleep, waking late, both of you delighted, tea on a tray, raisins in bed for it to chase about with one extended forefinger, chew and release and capture again, as you unsnap its prison-issue onesie, warm naked skin released to air. *Bwa ha ha.*

Your strange new feeling of misplaced pride persists as it bounces on the bed and throws its raisins on the floor, gets down by itself while you're in the kitchen, turns its happy face to you.

I know four couples like you, said the writer you met on the weekend.

Really?

Sure. Couples who have kids and don't live together.
And here you thought you were the only ones.

34. The Strain

THE BABY, SOFTLY AND SWEETLY PUT TO BED during the party, wakes up screeching. Urgent, stop press, priority, now. Obedient for once, even thankful to pay the bill for your fun (silken dress and stemmed glass, plates and conversation), you excuse and hasten. Already fumbling with strap you open the door and rush to darkened bedside. What could possibly be the trouble? Unwary, routine, you open the diaper, soaked no doubt, time for a change. And see it.

Shit.

Haven't we been through this before? Isn't this storyline getting a little old? Isn't this punchline, well, tired? You hold the baby over the toilet, it screams into your sateen belly, you feel part of some dark elemental process. Then you check its bottom and, yes, as it's straining and screaming, you actually do it.

You pull it out.

Not once. Not by accident as if you're wiping. But three times in all, discards in the bowl, like you're extracting tinsel from a cat, helping your Chihuahua that swallowed string, only you've never had to do this with a cat, you've never owned a dog that small. The indignity, the insupportable horror of it all.

35. Little People

AFTER A LONG TIME lying there playing with itself and not going to sleep it manages to throw itself off the bed headfirst, *thwap,* hear and rush, the baby's helpless, outraged cry. Later on the bus going to pick up your older daughter the baby is so tired it lolls and screams and sucks its fingers. *Told you,* you say, vicious, victorious. Triumph of a kind: your worst fears confirmed.

   In the café after school, another addict, tot in tow, sees your dense book of theory. One page turned since you arrived, true, but: *you can read?* she asks, disbelieving her eyes. Your older daughter has taken away the grimy miniature schoolbus from the infant and is acting out a pantomime. *Get off my bus,* she yells in a mock growl, sending Little People spinning. For once you are sympathetic to the man with the earset as, laughing, you tell her people are trying to work. *Yooou don't got no ID? Take this!* And another Bob or Ted is violently ejected while the baby watches wide-eyed.

36. Crimes, Evidence

bã'by *n.*, *& v.t.*: **1.** Set of chores to be done. **2.** Set of imperfections to be defended. *What is this?* your loved one and your daughter demand as one, when they catch sight of the baby. *Why is its chin so red?* Patiently you explain: the baby has sucked on its carrier until it is soaked, chafing its skin. You accept it, sort of: your responsibility.

The baby devours black beans, fisting them into an already-smeared face while watching you with round unblinking eyes. Could you bottle this essence of adorability, distil baby's ability to make you laugh in the midst of your litany of chores? Everyone should have one, should be puzzled by its screams and how it isn't going to sleep until, bending over solicitously, a little fairy punch, tell-tale smell, and opening its diaper catch it still in the act: uh-oh. *Oops. Guess the beans worked then, huh?* And the baby, screeching without regard for propriety, informing you that it hurts, some mismatch here between object and aperture, assist, rearrange: well, what is one to do except carry it around, still screaming, to let gravity assist in its work, and then remove the evidence afterwards? Don't mind me, I love doing laundry at bedtime, pinning up the last diaper that won't last anyway. At seven the next morning the doorbell rings, jolting you awake. You lie puzzled, wondering who at this hour, until you finally remember: your generous ex, bringing white shirts. A uniform for your upcoming doctoral examination back in England, at the university you attended two decades ago. White shirt, black skirt, tie: the very last requirement, in the list of them you ignored for so long. Twenty years ago, you didn't get that degree. Now you've fully circled, horse to fence, sailboat to dock: given your head, then keeled, patient, at last brought to book.

37. The Impending

BABY IS UP WHEN YOU ARRIVE at the babysitter's: a present you didn't want, but can't really take back, although it has crossed your mind. At home it stands up on the bed, ignoring your crabby suggestion that it's time to sleep. Peers over the headboard, wants to know what you're doing. *Work,* you explain. You and your loved one and the baby leave for Europe in a week, you have a thesis to—well, not defend, it's more nebulous than that, what else is new, in England; but your entire degree is riding on this, the outcome not known in advance, nor the impact of jet lag on the baby or on you, who suspect the worst.

Thus the shopping, to distract. You've run out of lipstick, all the tubes your friend the compulsive shopper passed on worn down to the rim. You need a rich beige, full price. None of these sale samples or mixed berries, but direct from the branded lacquered counter. You need the assurance, the obliteration of the you underneath for something worthy of the new doctoral degree you hope to finally achieve, this time. You'll buy matching polish, bring the baby along. What does it care? If it gets its hands on a disposable makeup applicator its whole day will be made.

But before you can even begin assembling supplies—sealing the barrels of rum, yo ho ho, stockpiling the lead-sealed tins purported to drive men mad—it scrapes its way over to you. Puts its hand on your leg. Tilts its head. Utters its cry: *Ma ma ma. Ma ma. Ma ma ma ma ma.* You suspect this is its word not for you but for comfort, two breasts, your smell, the timbre of your voice, that give it at once to understand: safety, rest. Here I put my head, open my mouth. Grapelike drops, quiver and fall. Life of Riley.

38. The Knowledge

HOW THE BABY STOPS CRYING when you put your mouth to its ear, speak to it low. The power of your chest, that even when you're not feeding it the cellular memory of those feeds, all of them, causes it to come to you, jam its fingers into its mouth, turn its head and nestle.

You watch it get out of bed. First it extends one leg, standing, feeling the air. Looks down, turns and gracefully lowers itself. Extending its reach. Stretching its range. Ability, and possibility. The baby's cry, *Ma ma*: faith, ever splintered and renewed. Demonstrations of favour: arms held out, smile of reward. Touching other people on the arm, lightly, while you hold it. When they reach for it, pulling quickly back, shrinking, little Violet. *Ma ma*.

At the rink the other mothers say to go ahead, take a turn on the ice while they watch the baby. Grateful beyond measure, you circle away. Gliding back, you see its open mouth, lips turned down, hear the dismal howl before it's even audible. Abandoned, crushed, ignored, denied, all your fault. The critic jeers. *You monster. You selfish. You, you, you. Why even have a baby, huh, if all you want to do is leave?*

Then home, stillness and quiet again. The baby's finicky fingers plucking at foodstuffs. The rare times it allows you to feed it still, opening its mouth, deciding. Its choked cry, the bathwater too hot or too cold. How well you two know each other, how this will stand you in stead.

39. Experimental Horror Movie

SLOW, DELIBERATE HAND-SLAPS BEHIND YOU. The suspense is killing, the silence that follows worse. Sure enough, in the vicinity of the bookcase, one touch, cascade and rip. To be removed, to be told no, to be provided with approved baby-safe toys: all mere distractions to be circumvented. And indeed, the moment you turn back to your screen the same smacks on the floor, same crawl, same case, same crash.

You must remember to write in its baby book, must be sure to record these precious passing moments before they glaze over in a haze of interrupted nights, a slick of curdling milk and its byproducts. Your days a slew of random household objects distinguished only by being within reach. Picked up again, scattered again, picked up again, scattered again. Good thing you have no brain cells left.

Month Eight: became more annoying.

Month Nine: discovered it could move. Became really super incredibly annoying.

Month Ten: take it on trust.

40. Here Comes the Airplane, Pbbt

THE BABY HAS LEARNED TO WAVE, splaying delighted fingers, smiling at itself, the spectacle. In the rows behind passengers react, lifting large hands. Wave, you tell the baby, bending to it. But the baby waves on a schedule known only to itself, will not be trained.

Now it has picked up the deplorable habit of spitting when whatever's offered is not to its taste, *pbbt, pbbt, pbbt,* a proceeding you both, in all innocence or as it later came to seem stupidity, initially encouraged. *Pbbt-bbt, awww, how cute, look at her,* and the belated realization.

Pfft. Pub-bubbub-bufft. The baby purses its lips and blows raspberries. Its mouth, choked by the food your loved one's levering in, emits a fine spray. *It's amazing how much you can get them to eat,* he says, *if you don't mind being spit on.* You try to wipe the worst of the squash from his tie, shirt, glasses, and face. *It's all right,* he says, displaying his usual splendid indifference. Shoulder puked, bed pooped, soaked pant leg: he remains somehow above it all, untouched, hovering over the fray. *All right for some,* you think sourly, remembering as ever his escape clause, emergency exit, ejection seat. Too bad you're so jealous, so spiteful, given that you planned it all.

41. Ruined

WHAT IS THIS, asks the don in disbelief. *What is this,* arrested just inside the door. Words failing, he gestures. Baby investigator, unheeding, scoots across the floor, collecting dust-puffed clues from under table leg and sofa seat. You should buy it a trenchcoat and hat, give it a magnifying glass to clutch.

You have always loved the Senior Common Room at your onetime Oxford college. French windows opening out onto the lawn, a big box of stationary on a table (you are writing thank-you notes, with your magenta pen). A coffret of ice, left moments ago, clouding now to metal bead and silver streak. Last time you were here you stole a lot of correspondence cards marked with the name of your college and were never invited back, which may or may not have been related. The sweet was a banana: the man next to you ate it with a knife and fork, as far from Darwin as he could get. Now you learn by asking (nobody would tell you unbidden, that's not the Oxbridge way) that you can sign up online to dine formally with the college fellows in the dining hall, at the big table on the raised dais. No need to wait for an invitation, these days.

I know, you say to the don in reply. You're wearing softest grey velvet, a perfect dress. You put it on, transformed. Turned to your loved one, your quarrel for once stilled. *I think it looks dowdy,* he said, and you pitied the partial vision of men.

I was surprised too, you continue. *I didn't think it would be allowed.*

Who said?

I asked in the Domestic Bursary, you say, ignoring the don's tone. And then another one enters and it's the same again: *what's this?* Same explanation, same patent disbelief. You go into the dining hall, through the passage only the dons use. Grace in Latin, rise and listen to call and response. Sitting again with palpable relief: whew, got that over. The undergraduates benched below, half-pints in plastic glasses by their plates.

You don't know that you are the senior woman and should start first. Instead you wait for the don at your right who has an amazing ability to tell a long story in a low voice that you can hear, you and the medical student across both laughing with polite relief, her better at it than you. The baby scampers around, is collected. *It's not that I never married,* says the don; *that's what they say when they mean "he's gay." I've had my heart broken so many times. I am what they call a lifelong bachelor.* Your loved one tells you later that the rest of the men gave up waiting for you finally and began to eat.

The baby is eating too, desperation food: forget the prohibitions on sugar and junk, anything to keep it quiet. You found the ultimate snack at the chemist's: puffed corn, Cheezie-style, rolled in dried carrot and described as "carrot sticks." The baby is crazy for them and who can blame it, they are quintessential junk, despite the earnest packaging promising the very opposite. On the plane back it lolls on his lap, watching The Backyardigans.

42. Removal Man

YOUR LOVED ONE HAS TAKEN THE BABY to his while you go home, ostensibly to work. It coos in the background, making exploratory noises, as you spar with him on the phone. The burn on its tongue a mystery but also, he is at pains to point out, a preventable injury. You agree, in tones of deepest sarcasm, that it certainly is. *Along with other such*, you add. Things have come to a pretty pass.

43. Double You

TWO SIDES OF THE EQUATION, asleep versus awake. The half-addled calculations all you're capable of, in this state. Add it up. It has catnapped for fifteen seconds in the stroller, has missed its usual morning nap, is in line for its second nap of the day, plus the first, that'd be great. Is at home in its own bed in its own sack, which it likes, has been nursed, is rubbing its eyes and crying, sucks its fingers, displays all the signs known to mother that it is ready to be abed. So please: someone, anyone, explain. Why does it sit up? Why the smile? Why the clapping hands? Your brain smoulders, heap of ash, slow fume, no solution here.

Earlier today you took it to city hall. You consider these occasions salutary, a sort of vitamin for council. And a jab for your offspring, inoculating them in good citizenship. Then you snuck onto the subway without paying, planning if you were caught—*Who me? I was just looking for the way down with the stroller!*—to use your white skin and middle-class airs, your enunciation, to get off. Two sides, same coin, take your pick: good mother or bad. Same as your own, slipping bars of paraffin under your infant dress for her batik work at home. You're short on laundry change again, cash poor as usual, six wet diapers you need to wash and a liner it has learned to pull off so that it stands bare-bottomed, clutching the edge of the couch. At least it won't soil another, until you catch sight of the evidence on the floor. Shit. Again.

You have a sad friend. Tonight she will visit and you'll give her the baby to hold, thinking it might be a comfort. *Wah, wah, wah,* the baby will go, face turning red and arms reaching out for you. You'll give in as always, but without grace, half hating it, ambivalent as ever. Open your arms, still, and accept your birthright: anchor, millstone with a monkey back.

44. You Were Told

ITS EAR STOPPED WITH CRYSTALLIZED WAX, you call the nurseline. The nurseline was established by the government to prevent people from going to the doctor. But every call, every symptom, elicits the same response.

Go to the doctor.

Yup, that sounds bad, see the doctor. You imagine the nurse, headpiece on, strolling around a gleaming kitchen island, one manicured hand selecting a piece of fruit from a heaped bowl.

So you trundle to the doctor only to be assured it's nothing, excrescences of wax apparently normal, the baby's ear clear. Doctor no doubt wondering why you didn't just call the nurseline: isn't that what it's for? Wednesday you attend a volunteer meeting for your favourite nonprofit. Look, it still exists, the outside world: people in clean clothes, speaking full sentences. Unfortunately you need to bring the baby, so you tell everyone it will not be much trouble, hah. It needed a nap when it arrived but perversely stayed awake instead, all these people to meet, then wanted you, and tried moving the chairs, and sat down and cried, and barely ate. Afterwards you notice that its ear appears to have simply exploded, wax everywhere. What's the point of calling the nurseline again, they'll simply tell you the usual, so you get a diagnosis from a friend: *if it was a burst eardrum,* she tells you, *there'd be blood, you'd know.*

45. The End

YOU MEET UP WITH HIM a week after your trip together. You bring the stroller so that the baby will not come between you when you open your arms, fold him to your chest. Magnanimous, embracing, look beyond, the big picture: that's you, generous to a fault. You've already overlooked so many defects in the baby, why not his?

You sit down. He offers coffee, breakfast, but for once you aren't hungry.

You're acting like there's nothing wrong with us, he says.

You bite back the sarcastic replies, settle for diplomacy. *There are certainly some things that need to change.* Sharing language. The avoidance of blame.

I want you out of my life, he says abruptly.

What about the baby? is all you can think to ask, your only disinterested ace.

I won't see the baby any more.

The poor, poor baby. Then you remember: this is how you wanted it, once. Ownership, a certificate even, clear line of responsibility, leading back to you.

46. Bolstered

YOU ALWAYS SUSPECTED that the baby's screams at night were payback, punishment even. You told yourself not to be so damn paranoid. After he left, though, after an hour of the baby teething, both of you with colds, your temper snapped. You hauled it up by the sack and carried it to its sister's room, temporarily empty while your older daughter stays with her dad. The older girl's half-height loft too far from the floor, so that even bolstered with pillows you had to worry about it throwing itself off. The baby screamed and cried.

Are you done?

Are you done now?

You swing open the door. The baby is discovered sitting up in a prayerful attitude, reproach personified. How very much it resents this treatment, what has it ever done, how could you. But behold if when you return it to your bed it isn't quiet, sucking its fingers and turning its head. So it was a tactic, a gambit, and you called its bluff. Mother 1.

No points for your innumerable weak attempts to put baby on a schedule, something you haven't managed since it was born. Someday it must be inserted into modern life, acquainted with the dismaying fact that one does not eat and wake when one wants but when outside forces dictate, not that you live that way yourself, but let that pass. This morning you're firm, have your usual conversation with yourself: *not going to put up, no way you'll,* and so on. You feed the baby at two, then when it wakes at five-thirty refuse to feed it again until six. It howls and is transferred to the sister's room and gets the idea and is returned, sucks its fingers and twists and rips at your hair (*No. No.*) Of course you can't sleep. You stumble up, trailing swamp goo: 5:45. More twisting, more finger-sucking, more pulling, more no's. Five-fifty-two. My goodness time goes slowly when trying to keep a baby and a pair of breasts, natural allies, one made for the others you might say, apart. Then six, what passes for six, you can't even remember if you kept to the filthy schedule last night, what's the point of this torture anyhow, who needs it, get a crib. The baby signalling ceaselessly, as if feeding was something you'd merely forgotten in the temporary amnesia of motherhood: ship to docking station, car to pump, *c'mon over, thisaway, pull 'er in.*

You lie there finally. Baby all suck, curled shrimp, cleave to you, amoeba, everything fined to a point and that point its mouth, while you slowly empty. Over and over, the ordinary miracle, full to spent. A size in a day, not one day but hundreds and thousands of them, all to be forgotten.

47. The Last Fight You Ever Had

YOU WAITED FOR HIM OUTSIDE the changerooms at the hotel gym. The baby tried pulling down the weights balanced on skinny iron rails. People passed murmuring *Aw look* and *How cute.*

After waiting forever and two days, calling his name into the men's, you used the phone outside, discovered him in your room. *What are you doing there?*

I came up.

You didn't even wait? You left us here?

You are incandescent with rage, lit, go flaming down the corridor.

What is wrong with you?

What is wrong with me? you spit. *I waited for you.*

Don't be ridiculous. Look at yourself. You're acting like a harridan. Most times you enjoy this sort of thing, the archaic words, but at this instant you couldn't care less.

He lies on the floor, his back still killing him from the transatlantic flight. You stomp around, accidentally graze his cheek with your foot, a circumstance he immediately turns to advantage. *Ow.*

What?

You kicked me. I was just lying here and you kicked me in the face.

I did not.

You most certainly did.

The baby, long past bedtime, stands up in its crib and cries,

adding to the general melee. He gets up and retrieves it. How
noble this makes him seem. He has a choice, not like you.

You slam the door, stalk downstairs, smoke a cigarette outside the lobby. Imagine going into one of the bars, ordering
a drink, your heartbreak and tragic air, the bartender you'll
impress with your story. Come back late, stinking, leave him
holding the bag, the baby, show him what it feels like to wait
for once. You go upstairs ten minutes later as you knew you
would. Grand gestures never your thing. Might as well give
it another feed, another chance to sleep through the night for
the first time ever, another piece of you.

48. Who Now?

YOU ENGAGE A SITTER, a lady from another country. *She does things differently,* your daughter tells you when you return.

And indeed the sitter proceeds to enlighten you about the baby's requirements. *She needs two naps, not three.*

Uh-huh, you agree.

Ten and three.

Uh-huh. How relieved you are, to have someone else tell you what to do! Only when she's gone do you remember: the baby cannot nap at three, when you are picking up your older daughter.

She drank a bag of breastmilk, the sitter continues. And when you walk in the door (your older daughter hovering to let you in): *You probably want to feed her now.* You find the lady's bossiness comforting, even though she's only a few years older than you. Wish she would take you in hand, all of you. Later you notice she's done your dishes, and feel a gratitude out of all proportion. If she wasn't already gone you would take her hand and wring it.

It was your first time without the baby, without him: a whole day, at a stretch. You took the water route. Even that little time on the harbour, surrounded by squirming children looking out the front window at the vista, was too much. Made you remember, and misted you over, like weather coming in.

49. Fell Down the Stairs

THE BABY HAS A BLACK EYE. The worst part is it's all your fault. You put it outside your door, got your coat, wandered through one more time to check the innumerable missing. Keys, diaper, plastic bag that you reuse, wallet, cards, snack for you, for it, just in case you're stranded on a desert island, in the middle of the city. What else? Always something else.

Thump. *Waah.* You rushed out, picked it up, smothered and comforted. Then you saw: evidence. At least he's no longer here to sneer at your undeniable dereliction, to turn away with silent reproach.

50. One Last Wave

ONE DAY YOUR OLDER DAUGHTER loses all restraint. *Take it away,* she roars, *send it back, I'm sick of it.* She tells you that when you leave them with a sitter the baby cries and cries, despite the sitter's efforts, until the sister comes to comfort it. Those nights when you are gone she complains that she has not a moment's peace. *Don't leave me,* she screams, *take me with you, I don't care if the meeting is boring, I'll sit through it.*

You sympathize really, but imagine your duty instead is to pretend to outrage, point out her own small transgressions. *How would you like it if we'd given you away, thrown you out,* you ask. *What a terrible thing to say.* When really you perfectly understand, having had the like impulse innumerable times.

51. Happy

BABY'S FIRST BIRTHDAY. You bake carrot cake into a breast-shaped dome, let it drink sparkling apple juice from a flute. *Evidence,* someone says, taking a picture. *Social services. I don't think I'll be there,* he told you over the phone. It looks up at you, wide eyes unblinking. Trusting little tub. Opens its mouth, makes unintelligible noises. Scientists claim this a precursor to speech. Could have fooled you. But you've read the baby books, grasped the facts. One more year to go, before it attains the intelligence of a terrier.

52. Reckoning

YOU ARE NOT THE MOST PATIENT OF PEOPLE. You are perhaps the most impatient. You like always to be at the front of a line, cut ahead of the lame and halt as they shuffle feebly, maneuvering walkers and crutches. You'll get through first, you tell yourself, leave the way open for them. You're quick in your movements, interrupt constantly, and start to fidget when dawdling.

You're always late, fifteen minutes or so, out of your incessant fear of being bored; you'd rather have to rush and make it up on the way than arrive early with nothing to do. You have no regard for the inconvenience this causes others, except as you're already on your way to heartily regret it as you'd regret a natural disaster, nothing of your making.

You cut corners, you're always in a hurry, opening and discovering things you haven't done right, having to go back, although you know you'd save time if you slowed down, did them right the first time;

Are you done yet, you say to the baby, practically jiggling it, *there, that's enough,* already buttoning your shirt, pushing it away, so that it learns to feed in five minutes flat when the books say it should take twenty;

You cannot stand to play with the baby, anything but that, fate worse than death, to manipulate its little figurines, use that sing-songy voice, attempt to engage its interest in essentially brain-killing (for you, anyhow) activity;

You shout too much, raise your voice even when you know

it's no good, teaching the baby nothing except to shout back. You must be obeyed, your tone turns harsh if you aren't, instantly. You knit your brows, practically stamp your foot, Wicked Witch-like, West;

You are extremely vain, and always want to be impeccably dressed, despite the fact that everything you own has been passed from somebody who felt sorry for your destitute, worn state and thus is slightly too big or small, or for someone older or younger; and if from your own meager stock is spattered with bicycle grease, torn from where you feverishly ripped it away from some caught protuberance, or creeps up over your still-bulging flesh. Your vanity even extends to the baby, sinfully so. You would like to be dressed the same, or at least in the same colours and approximations: matching pink polos, a beige pair of pants to your beige skirt. But of course the organization this demands is such that it might as well be an injunction to speak Swahili, so impossible is it;

You love to shock in the manner of a teenager, and are always making inappropriate comments in a bid for attention, and since some of these nowadays perforce involve the baby they are probably even more unwise than usual;

You take pride in ridiculous things, like how you take the baby everywhere, and you expect that everyone should be as pleased and admiring of your pluck as you, not so secretly, are yourself; and when they aren't, but instead find your presumption irritating or even obnoxious, you are surprised and dismayed anew no matter how many times it happens;

Like all parents, you believe everyone should adore your baby, admire its cleverness, recognize and fall for its charm, and if they don't you quietly pity them, while at the same time congratulating yourself on how broad-minded you are, not to write them off at once as the insensitive monsters they've demonstrated themselves to be.

A lifetime of this to come, you realize, see-saw and echo. Her incessant questions (repeat, repeat) to come with speech, your eroding calm and rising quick fury over the ebb of the day, over and over, even after the milk finally taps shut. Then the sullen subsiding into mutual hostility, covert now, in her teens, and at last, eons later (if you're lucky), the rise again, to human relations. A lifetime of it, all mothers, all children, all the blame in the world, you and her, particular and constant, just like everyone else, just what you needed, happy at last.

Photo: Julia Saunders

Carellin Brooks is the author of *Wreck Beach* (2007), a social geography of the most beautiful nude beach in the world, and *Every Inch a Woman* (2005), an academic exploration of the phallic-woman motif in contemporary texts. She has edited two collections, *Bad Jobs* (1998) and, with co-editor Brett Josef Grubisic, *Carnal Nation* (2000).